PRIVATE EYE

Cartoon Library 8

The jokes of

Also published in this series:
Michael Heath (Volumes I and 2),
Hector Breeze, Larry, Martin Honeysett,
Barry Fantoni and John Glashan.

Published in Great Britain 1976 by
Private Eye Productions Limited,
34 Greek Street, London W1.
In association with Andre Deutsch Limited,
105 Great Russell Street, London WC1.

© Pressdram Limited
SBN 233 96833 4
Most of the following cartoons were drawn specially for
this book, others were first seen in Private Eye.

Designed by Peter Windett.
Printed in Great Britain by Halstan & Co. Ltd.,
Amersham, Bucks.

"In bed he just lies there"

"I'd better ring off now, Mabel. My arm is going a funny colour"

"John, was it 1921 or 1922 that I was ravished by all those Tartars?"

"Henry. I'm afraid we're through. I've had the lock changed"

"O.K., kid, hand over the message"

"Ah, Jenkins, the Board has brought your retiring age forward thirty-five years"

"I miss the children"

"You know what they say, Job. Everyone has a Book in him"

"How about us going bump in the night?"

"Theirs has been a phenomenal growth rate"

"Poor devil – stage fright"

"Don't mind me. I'm from the Bayeux Tapestry"

"...and never speak to strange walruses and carpenters"

"All right, Burnaby, you get the raise!"

*"It doesn't mean **anything**. It's just the state creating employment"*

"I granted his death wish"

"They never did fight fair."

"It's an invitation from the Brontes. They're having another funeral"

"It's magnificent but is it ballet?"

"Just how tall do you want to be, Otto?"

"Last year it was blackbirds"

"I'm either drinking too much or the dawn comes up like thunder"

"Tomorrow will be in the low seventies with scattered showers"

"Once a year it's our turn to wait on the servants"

24

1

2

3

4

"I've never seen an octopus this far inland before"

"Does this damned thing have a reverse?"

"Long knives, you fool!"

"It's for a budgie"

"I know they said don't call them, they'd call you, but that was 30 years ago"

"... *the dipping of a hundred oars, the ritual beat of the drum, the exciting crack of the whip, the community feeling. You'll be back, Abdul. You'll be back*"

"This looks like the end of Monarchy as we have known it"

"One of the great actor-managers"

"He was one of the finest stand-up comics in the business"

"Why, Mr Faberge, you've surpassed yourself!"

"All in favour of the motion say Craunck Craunck!"

"It's hand operated by four thousand souls in torment"

"That money wrapped up in a five pound note — it's mine! All mine!"

37

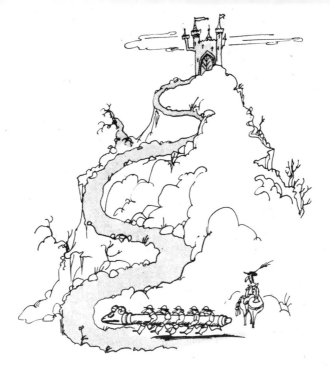

"Not yet, you fools. Don't start running yet!"

"Same order every day. Ten million curries"

"He wasn't trying to catch the auctioneer's eye. He was dropping down dead"

"It's something new in a wig. It goes grey and begins to fall out"

"Guess who's begatting!"

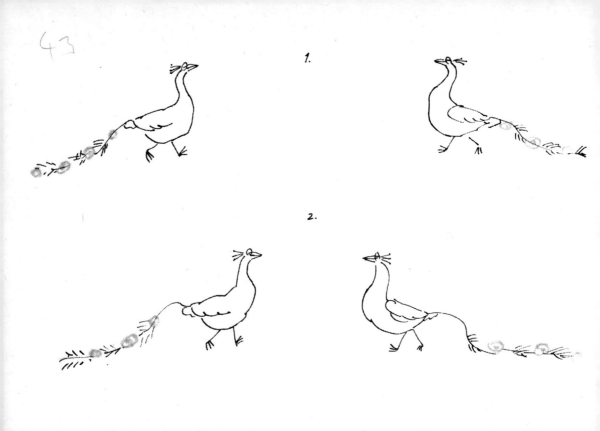

1.

2.

3.

4.

"Sorry"

*"Now that's what **I call** inscrutable"*

"Dumkopf!"

*"Don't be foolish, Stephenson, you'll never get **that** to fly"*

"Paint was hardly dry..."

"If there's one thing I hate it's gold coins in bed"

"It's going to be one of those Sundays"

"He won the Nobel Prize for failing to win the Nobel Prize more often than anyone else"

"Basically I like it but take out the carrot"

"*For heaven's sake, Augustus, they haven't even started yet!*"

"Into the Valley of Death rode the 600, oh poor fellow, into the Valley of Death rode the 599 . . ."

"Probably booby-trapped"

"There must be some mistake. We're trying to contact Lord Baden-Powell"

"Pull the other one, it's got bells on it"

"Brilliant technique but he has nothing to say"

"You are the proud possessor of a great name, son. Go out and tarnish it"

"The daily garlic count is up ten per cent"

"Battersby's in his second childhood."

*"There's always **one** who has to spoil it for everybody else"*

"Whatever happened to the old tea-party?"

63

"I'm afraid it's the Change of Life. She tried to jump over the moon"

"*I intend to open some kind of shop when I get out of here*"

"I'm sorry, but can you come back tomorrow? The Oracle has wind"

"He's under terrific pressure."

"Get the hell out of it, this is a White Man's Grave!"

69

"*Is it me, or is it raining?*"

70

"*I'm sorry but this monastery is closed for the Reformation*"

"*Sometimes, Miss Cooper, I think there must be something around here that **eats** paperclips*"

"Underneath he's probably quite a nice fellow"

"Things are going from bad to worse with the Barlows"

"A King's Ransom is down 12½ points"

"It gets me there and it gets me back"

"He can't stand Robin Day"

"Here out West, son, we call a spade a spade"

"You never truly cared, Roger. To you I was just so much ballast"

"My husband's in hi-jacking"

"It's the mating season and I have absolutely nothing to wear"

"To you it may be just a windmill but to me it's The System!"

7

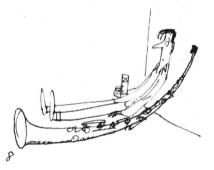

8

"Door!"

"Would you like the plain or the Greetings Death Certificate?"

"Start naming names or we fill up the moat!"

"He's working on his masterpiece. A treble entendre"

"You know what they say. You can never get enough of the stuff"